Numbed!

David LUBAR

MILLBROOK PRESS • MINNEAPOLIS

Millbrook Press
A division of Lerner Publishing Group, Inc.
241 First Avenue North
Minneapolis, MN 55401 USA

For reading levels and more information, look up this title at www.lernerbooks.com.

Main body text set in Goudy Oldstyle Std. Regular 14/24.
Typeface provided by Adobe Systems.

Library of Congress Cataloging-in-Publication Data

Lubar, David.
        Numbed! / by David Lubar.
             pages   cm
        Summary: When a robot at the math museum zaps their math skills, sixth-grader Logan and his mischievous friend, Benedict, must pass a series of math challenges to retrieve their knowledge.
        ISBN 978–1–4677–0594–3 (trade hard cover : alk. paper)
        ISBN 978–1–4677–1699–4 (eBook)
        [1. Mathematics—Fiction.] I. Title.
PZ7.L96775Nu 2013
[Fic]—dc23   2012048863

Manufactured in the United States of America
2 – SB – 7/15/14

For Guy, Robin, Erin, Ryan, and Kevin Connelly, for a number of reasons

CONTENTS

CHAPTER
5 + 4 − 8

"I wish we could go somewhere interesting," Benedict said as we got off the bus with the rest of our class.

"It won't be that bad," I said.

"Are you kidding, Logan? It's math! It's bad enough we have to do fifty zillion homework problems every day. And now, we get dragged here?" He flung his arm in the direction of the

Mobius Mathematics Museum. It was shaped like the top half of a planet, with a giant, twisted steel ring circling a dome of colored glass. The ring was just high enough above the ground that people could walk under it and thick enough that I could probably walk inside of it, assuming it was hollow. The dome had craters and spikes scattered across the surface. Huge numbers, symbols, and equations were painted on it in random places in pink, yellow, red, and purple.

"It's kind of a cool building," I said, trying to get Benedict to calm down before our teacher, Ms. Fractalli, decided to make him stay on the bus. It was only our second month of sixth grade, and she'd already kept him after school twelve times. That's not even counting all the times he had to miss recess.

"No," Benedict said. "The natural history museum is cool. They have all sorts of dead things. I guarantee, this is going to be awful." He jammed his Ravens hat tighter on his head. He always wore it for at least a week after his mom cut his hair.

Ms. Fractalli turned around and said, "Benedict, I expect you to behave. And take off that hat before we go inside." Then she pointed at me and flicked her finger toward herself, like she was tickling the belly of a tall dog. "Logan, come here."

I tapped my chest. "Me?"

She double flicked. "You."

"Hah—you're in trouble," Benedict said as he stuffed his hat in his back pocket.

I ignored him and walked over to our teacher.

She bent down, lowered her voice, and said, "I'm counting on you to see that Benedict behaves."

"Me?" This time, I didn't tap any part of my body.

"You." This time, she didn't flick any fingers.

"But I can't make him behave," I said. She might as well have asked me to make the wind stop blowing.

"Sure, you can. You're his friend. He listens to you. As I said, I'm counting on you. I know you won't let me down." She turned away before I could figure out how to convince her that whatever Benedict ended up doing, it wouldn't be my fault.

"I'll try to keep you out of trouble," Benedict said when I got back over to him. "But you're going to have to stick close."

"Thanks. I'll do my best."

Our class streamed beneath the ring and through the front entrance of the museum. There was a big digital counter hanging from the ceiling just past the door. It was the same kind they use at the deli in the supermarket—but with a lot more digits. The numbers clicked forward, going up by two as Benedict and I went in.

"I count!" Benedict said, pointing up at the display.

He ran outside, slid to a halt, and let out a screech like a skidding car in a video game. He spun around and raced back. "And I count again," he said.

He did this twice more, bumping the count higher each time, before I could grab his shoulder and say, "Come on, the class is getting ahead of us."

We caught up with the end of the line as it reached the other side of the lobby. I noticed a video running on a big screen overhead. A man held up a strip of paper. "The Mobius strip is easy to make but amazing to explore," he said. He gave the paper a twist and then taped the ends together, making a loop.

He took a pencil and started to draw a line on the outside. "It only has one side," he said.

Our group moved out of the lobby, so I didn't see the rest of the video. Ms. Fractalli led us down a hallway toward an area called the Chamber of Fractions.

Just then, Benedict grabbed my arm and shouted, "Look!"

With his other hand, he pointed at a sign hanging from the middle of a thick rope that blocked an opening on the left side of the hall-way. I could see a flight of stairs past the opening, heading down to the basement. The sign read:

RESTRICTED EXPERIMENTAL AREA
CLOSED TO THE PUBLIC
ABSOLUTELY NO VISITORS ALLOWED

"Awesome!" Benedict said. "They wouldn't put up a sign if it was really a secret. They want people to go there."

"That's ridiculous." I grabbed Benedict's shoulder. "If they wanted people to go down there, they'd say so on the sign."

"Then everyone would go," he said. "They want people, but only the ones who are smart enough to figure that out. Like us. Let's go."

Before I could say anything, he'd slipped from my grip, ducked under the rope, and raced down the stairs. I found myself alone, listening to the fading squeak of his sneakers on the tile floor and imagining what Ms. Fractalli would do to both of us when Benedict got in trouble down there.

If I didn't chase after him, I'd get blamed. But the last time I'd chased him anywhere, I ended up getting punished. That had not been fun.

"I hope this time is different," I muttered to myself.

I had no idea I was about to get my wish. This time would definitely be different—mostly because it would be a whole lot worse.

CHAPTER
1 + 1

I checked over my shoulder to make sure Ms. Fractalli wasn't watching. Then I slipped under the rope and hurried down the steps. They led me to a long hallway with doors on both sides. I found Benedict in the third room on the left. He wasn't alone.

A small man wearing a lab coat was hunched over a workbench. His frizzy hair was just starting to turn gray at the sides, but his mustache was still dark black. My jaw dropped as I stared across the workbench. It wasn't the man who surprised me. It was the robot. "Awesome!" I said. I love electronics.

"Yeah, awesome," Benedict said.

The robot had all kinds of flashing lights on it, like an old-fashioned pinball machine. It had a pair of video camera lenses for eyes and small microphones for ears. It had jointed arms that ended in three-pronged claws like those machines at the amusement park where you try to win a toy. The robot didn't have any legs or wheels. I guess it wasn't supposed to walk or roll anywhere. Or maybe it wasn't finished. The man had a whole table full of parts in front of him.

"I agree. It's definitely awesome," he said. "Or

it will be, once I work out a couple of glitches."
He smiled at us. I relaxed a bit when I realized
he didn't seem to mind that we were there.

"What is it?" Benedict asked.

"A new interactive exhibit—Cypher, the
Number Cruncher. We're developing a whole
section of new math experiences." The man
held out his hand. "I'm Dr. Thagoras. I just
started working here last month."

"Cypher must know a zillion numbers," I said.

Dr. Thagoras laughed. "Actually, he only
knows two numbers. Make that two digits. But
that's all he needs."

"No way," Benedict said. "Even Logan's dog
knows more than that."

"Cypher's memory is nothing but switches."
Dr. Thagoras reached over to the wall and

flicked the lights off and then back on. "Off and on—that's all he has. Or 1 and 0. If *on* means "1" and *off* means "0," you have every number you need, as long as you have enough switches."

"No, you don't," Benedict said. "You don't have the number fifteen. Or ten thousand."

Dr. Thagoras grabbed a piece of paper and a pen. "Let's back away from switches and start with the simplest system of all." He made a bunch of short slashes on the page.

/////////////////

"There you have fifteen," he said. "I'd need more paper and a lot more time to write down ten thousand this way."

"That's not fifteen," Benedict said. "That's just silly."

"No, that's just unary—counting by ones,"

Dr. Thagoras said. "It's not very useful, except for counting small quantities of things. But Cypher uses binary. So do computers and video games. It's much more useful—especially if you have billions of switches. Wait—I have a device that will make everything a lot clearer. It's for one of the new exhibits. I'll go get it."

He hit a switch on the front of the robot. The lights on its body went dark, and the head slumped forward. Dr. Thagoras hopped off his stool and headed out the door. "I'll be right back. Don't touch anything."

No! I spun toward Benedict, but it was too late. Those words—*don't touch anything*—had already set him into action.

"I think *on* is more fun than *off*. Who wants to be a zero when you can be *numero uno*?" He flipped a switch on the robot's chest. The lights flashed to life, and the head tilted back up.

"He told us not to touch it," I said.

"Nah, he told you. Not me. I'm really good with electronics." Benedict stabbed at several more buttons. "I wonder what else it can do."

I tried to distract him before he broke something. "Hey—you were wrong. This place isn't boring."

"Most of it is still boring. Come on—a Chamber of Fractions? Give me a break." He grabbed a knob on the robot's neck and twisted it. "I hate math."

The robot turned its head toward us. "I love numbers." Its voice reminded me of the GPS Mom and Dad use in the car. Dad talks back to it—especially when he thinks it gave him the wrong directions. But when he ignores the GPS and drives the way he thinks is right, we always get lost.

The robot kept talking. "Numbers are wonderful. I am numbers. Numbers are my world. I live in a digital domain. I am a binary being. One, two, four, eight, sixteen."

"It loves *words* way too much," Benedict muttered to me. Then he turned toward the robot and said, "You can't love numbers. And you sure can't love math." He jabbed it in the chest, hitting another button.

"I love numbers. I love numbers. I love numbers." The robot repeated the words faster and faster. It started to sound like "Olive numbers" and then "lumbers," and after that, it didn't sound much like any words at all. It sounded like a car trying to start on a very cold morning. Smoke drifted from the robot's ears. It smelled like the time I'd left my plastic ruler too close to the toaster.

"Oh dear!" Dr. Thagoras rushed back in and switched off the robot. "You seemed to have found a flaw in its programming. I think I'd better grab the fire extinguisher. Hold this. And don't touch anything." He shoved a small box with three on-off switches and three lights into my hands and raced back out.

"Don't leave!" I shouted. "And stop saying that!"

As soon as Dr. Thagoras vanished down the hall, Benedict smirked and said, "I've got a few more things to tell this robot." He reached for the button.

"No!"

I tried to grab his arm, but I wasn't fast enough.

"Numbers are stupid!" Benedict shouted at the robot. "Even robots are boring when all they talk about is numbers."

I expected another rapid stream of words from the robot or maybe a screech like Dad's desktop computer at work made when the fan broke. Instead, the robot spoke in a low voice. It was almost a whisper. And it was so calm and cold, it made me shiver.

"You are wrong about numbers. You must be numbed."

It raised an arm. I heard a hum. A bolt of energy shot out from the center of its claw and hit Benedict in the middle of his forehead. Benedict started to twitch. I heard another hum.

The robot was getting ready to zap him again.

"Look out!" I leaped at him and gave him a shove, pushing him away from the zapping energy—and putting myself right in line to get hit.

Something exploded against the side of my head. I got so dizzy that I dropped to the floor. I had the weirdest feeling, like air was rushing out of my head. Everything grew dark, except for little bits of light that swirled like fireflies as they flew away from me. When one shot past my eyes, I saw it was a tiny, glowing number. It was as if someone had made shiny confetti out of a shredded math test. They were all numbers and symbols, escaping from my head and passing right through the walls and ceiling.

As the last glowing number left the room, the darkness took over and I passed out.

CHAPTER
6 ÷ 2

When I woke up, Dr. Thagoras was leaning over me, splashing water on my face from a glass. I sat up and looked at Benedict just as he opened his eyes.

"Are you boys all right?" Dr. Thagoras asked.

I touched the side of my head. It felt okay. "I'm fine," I said.

Benedict pointed at the robot. "But that thing is dangerous."

"I don't understand it," Dr. Thagoras said. "Cypher has never done anything like this before. Something must have completely overloaded the central logic circuits."

"We'd better catch up with our class," I said. I figured, if I got lucky, we'd be able to join them before Ms. Fractalli realized we were missing. And I didn't want to stay down there long enough for the doctor to figure out that Benedict could overload pretty much anyone's logic circuits.

"Don't you want to see the exhibit?" Dr. Thagoras asked. He picked up the box from the floor and started flipping the three switches, making the lights go on and off. "Look—I can count from zero to seven. If I had four switches, I could count to fifteen."

"You can count on us getting out of here," Benedict said as he fled from the room.

"We'll check it out next time." I hurried after Benedict. I'd had enough switches and lights and numbers for a while.

We went upstairs and managed to slip back with our class just as they were leaving the Chamber of Fractions and heading for the Amazing History of Zero diorama. I didn't pay much attention to the museum exhibits during the rest of the visit. I was feeling a bit fuzzy. I figured I hadn't totally recovered from getting zapped.

After we'd visited the rest of the museum, we got on the bus and headed back to school. Since we'd spent most of the school day in the math museum, we had a reading lesson for the rest of the afternoon.

"Be sure to study your math tonight and tomorrow," Ms. Fractalli said when the bell rang. "We're having a big test on Wednesday. And because you all behaved so well in the museum, I've decided to give you a special reward. If the average test score is high enough, you'll earn a class party with ice cream sundaes."

That produced cheers from everyone except Benedict. "Now I have to study really hard, or everyone will blame me," he said.

"Come on," I said. "You won't do that badly."

"I hope you're right," Benedict said. "I don't want to go through life being known as the kid who killed the ice cream party."

"Hold on. I think she needs me." I watched Ms. Fractalli as she searched for her key. She kept stuff locked in a cabinet near the door, but she was always losing the key.

I walked over to her desk, looked at it, looked under it, looked at it again, and then spotted the key inside her empty coffee cup. "There it is," I said. I could have gone right to the coffee cup, but I figured it seemed more impressive this way.

"Thank you, Logan." She took the key and opened the cabinet.

"Maybe you can ask her to give me a break on the math test, since you're always finding the key," Benedict said.

"I don't think that would work," I said. "Come on, let's get going. My mom's probably waiting outside."

My mom was picking Benedict and me up. She had to shop for my grandma's birthday present and had promised we could ride along to the mall. Luckily, she wouldn't drag us to the boring stores. We'd get to go off on our own.

But first, she took us to the food court on the top floor and bought us frozen juice drinks. The orange-banana Slush Monster with extra honey is about as perfect a drink as you can get. It has enough fruit to make Mom happy and enough sugar to keep me hoppy.

"Okay, Logan, I'll meet you and Benedict right here in two hours," my mom said. "Don't be late."

"We won't." I'd learned that lesson the hard way. The one time I didn't meet Mom on time, she'd had them announce my name over the mall loudspeakers. Talk about embarrassing. Especially the part where they described me as a "lost little boy."

"Have fun," she said.

"We will. Thanks." I turned to Benedict. "Where do you want to go?"

He slurped a long drink through his straw before answering. He'd gotten coconut cream with extra hazelnut syrup. "Well, she told us to have fun, so that means the game store, right?"

"For sure." We headed toward the escalator. I took a big drink too and then wished I hadn't as a sharp pain jabbed my forehead. "Brain freeze!" I shouted.

"Hah, you weakling. That never happens to me." Benedict drained the rest of his drink in one huge slurp. "See? I'm invulnerable." Then he grabbed his forehead and screamed, "Owwww!"

"At least it doesn't last long," I said.

By the time we reached the next level, my

pain was gone. Benedict had stopped howling too. He glanced at his watch as we headed for the ground floor and then frowned and looked at me. "What time are we meeting your mom?"

"In two hours," I said. "You heard her."

"Yeah, I know it's in two hours, but what time will that be?"

"Are you kidding? You really did freeze your brain." I checked my watch. It was 4:15. I opened my mouth to tell Benedict the answer. My mouth remained open, but no sound came out.

"You too?" Benedict asked.

"Me too." I stepped off the escalator at the bottom. *It's four fifteen*, I thought. *In two hours, it will be . . .*

I had no idea what the answer was or how to figure it out. I couldn't even think of the right way to get started, no matter how hard I tried. "I can't do the math," I said. The pain was gone. My brain wasn't frozen anymore. But there was something wrong with my mind.

"What do we do?" Benedict asked.

I looked back up toward the food court. My mom wouldn't be happy if we weren't there when we were supposed to be. "I guess we have to go back right now and wait up there for her," I said.

"It's that robot at the museum," Benedict said. "He did this to us."

I remembered his words: *You need to be numbed.* That's what was wrong with us. Our minds had been numbed. "I wonder how bad it is. Ask me a math problem."

"What's 1 + 1?" Benedict said.

"I have no idea. Nine?" I guessed. "Could it be nine?"

"How would I know?" Benedict said.

"Good point."

"This is worse than when you could only speak in puns," he said.

"A lot worse."

"Especially since you weren't the only person to get zapped. I'm numbed too. I knew you'd get me in trouble."

"Me?" I shouted. "You're the one who got us numbed, pushing all those buttons on the robot."

We argued about it all the way back to the food court. The only thing we agreed about was that we had to return to the museum as soon as possible to see if Dr. Thagoras could help us.

We grabbed seats at an empty table. But Benedict didn't sit for long. "I need a cinnamon bun," he said. "We could be waiting here forever. I can't wait that long without a snack."

He pulled out his wallet and walked over to the GooeyBun stand. I watched him as he looked up at the prices, then looked down at his wallet and then back up at the prices. He kept doing that.

Finally, I went over. "What's wrong?"

He handed me his wallet. "I don't know if I have enough money."

He had some dollar bills. I tried to count them, but I didn't know how. So I took them all out of the wallet, went up to the counter, and asked the guy behind it, "Is this enough for a GooeyBun?"

"You can't count?" the guy asked.

"We just had our eyes examined," Benedict said. "We're not supposed to use them for another hour."

The guy frowned, but he took the money and counted it. I watched what he did, but it still didn't make sense. He smiled and said, "It's just enough."

He handed me the cinnamon bun. I gave it to Benedict.

"Thanks," Benedict said. He turned to the guy and asked, "Shouldn't I get some change?"

"Oh, yeah. Sure." The guy reached into the penny dish and gave Benedict some coins. "Here you go."

Benedict stared at the pennies. I tugged at his arm. "Just be happy you got the bun." We had no idea how much Benedict had paid. But I had the feeling the guy behind the counter had given himself a big tip.

We went back to the table, where Benedict ate his bun and I wondered how many other things would be impossible if I couldn't do math. I glanced at my watch again. I knew what time it was. I guess that didn't need math skills—just reading. But I had no idea what time it had been five minutes ago or what time it would be an hour from now. I looked around at the menu boards in the food court. I could read the prices. I could see what a burger cost and what fries cost. But I had no idea what it would cost if I wanted both.

"We really need to go to the museum," I said.

"Mmmffffflllgpp," Benedict said, nodding in

agreement as he chewed a mouthful of his cinnamon bun.

"This really is all your fault," I said.

"Nnnmmmglubgulp."

I thought about getting a bun for myself, but I really didn't want to go through the terror of buying it. I never would have guessed it would feel so awful to lose my math skills. Happily, Benedict broke off a big piece of his bun to share with me. That helped pass the time.

"Logan, Benedict, I'm proud of you," Mom said when she met us. She glanced at her watch. "You're here right on time."

I checked my own watch. It was 6:15. Not that those numbers really meant anything to me.

That's when Benedict did something I'd never seen him do before—not even when he got smacked in the face with a soccer ball in gym class or the time he'd touched the coal stove in the Benjamin Franklin exhibit at the history museum to see if it really was red hot.

"Waaaaaaahhhhh!!!!" Benedict started to cry.

CHAPTER
$(6 \times 2) \div (4 - 1)$

Like all mothers, my mom has an instant reaction to crying. "What's wrong, dear?" she asked, kneeling by Benedict and putting an arm around him.

"I forgot my hat," Benedict said. He sniffed and wiped his nose with the back of his hand. His face was all scrunched up, but I didn't see any tears.

Mom glanced around the food court. "I'm sure it's here, somewhere. If not, we can check with lost and found. Do you remember which stores you went to?" Then she frowned and said, "Wait. You weren't wearing a hat when I picked you up at school."

It amazed me how moms seem to notice unimportant stuff like that.

"I left it at the math museum today," Benedict said. "Can we go there?"

Wow—I guess he'd really left his hat there. But until he realized we needed to go back to the museum, he didn't care.

"Don't worry. We'll go right there. I hope they're still open."

We followed Mom to the car. She drove us to the museum and pulled up by the front entrance.

I was glad to see the place hadn't closed yet.

"I'll be right back," Benedict said as he slid off his seat. "Come on, Logan."

I followed him in. We still had our badges from that morning. We ducked under the rope with the Restricted Experimental Area sign, went down the stairs, and found Dr. Thagoras in his lab. He was attaching wheels to the bottom of his robot. Benedict's hat was sitting on a stool.

I wrinkled my nose. The smell of burned plastic was still pretty strong. Dr. Thagoras didn't look up. I cleared my throat.

"Well, hello again," he said. "Are you still here? That's wonderful. There is so much to see upstairs."

"We left, but we came back." I pointed at the robot. "That thing numbed us."

The robot turned its head toward me. But it didn't raise a claw. I got ready to duck, just in case.

"Numbed?" Dr. Thagoras asked.

"Yeah, numbed!" Benedict shouted as he snatched his hat. "We can't add, thanks to that stupid thing."

"Stupid?" the robot said. "I'm stupid? I can add. Can you add? Who's stupid? I know 9 + 8 = 17. Seventeen is a prime number. Nine is a square, made of 3 × 3. Eight is a cube, made of 2 × 2 × 2. I love numbers. When you take 9 × 8, you get 72. Add the 7 to the 2, you get 9 again. That's awesome! Take 9 × 9 and you get 81. Add the 8 and the 1, you get right back to 9. Super awesome!"

"Hold on." Dr. Thagoras turned off the robot. "Cypher does tend to go off on tangents." He chuckled, as if this was some sort of joke, then said, "Tangents," again.

I relaxed as Cypher's head drooped forward, because nothing it said about the numbers made any sense to me. And because, now that it was turned off, it definitely couldn't zap us again.

"This is serious," Dr. Thagoras said. "You boys are telling me you've lost the ability to do simple addition."

"Yup," I said. "I don't even know what 1 + 1 is."

"I couldn't even figure out how to buy a GooeyBun," Benedict said.

"This can't be . . ." Dr. Thagoras glanced at the robot. "Any effect should have been temporary. Cypher runs on a very low voltage. Have you been exposed to any other sort of head trauma?"

I thought back. "We both had brain freeze."

"Oh, dear," Dr. Thagoras said. Give me a moment." He pulled a huge book from a shelf behind his desk and started flipping around to different pages. After a while, he shut the book. "That explains it. The zap should have faded by evening, but the freeze made it permanent."

"Permanent?" Benedict said.

"You have to fix us," I said.

"Hmmmm." Dr. Thagoras stared at me for a moment and then glanced down the hall. "Well, there's one thing that might work. If you can get through the tests in the matheteria, that will reboot your skills. The reboot could be enough to overcome the freeze." He hopped off his stool and headed down the hall.

"But how can we pass math tests if we can't do math?" I asked.

"Anyone can do math inside the matheteria," he said. "It generates a special field that makes it easier for people to work with numbers. It was designed to help people overcome their fear of math. I've never encountered numbed brains before, but I'm pretty sure the field can handle even that. I guess we'll find out in a minute."

"And then we'll be fixed?" I asked.

"That's up to you," he said. "The effect will fade once you're outside the matheteria, unless you pass the tests."

We followed him all the way to the end of the hallway. He let us into a room that had a door on our left, a door on our right, and a door at the far end, marked Maintenance.

Dr. Thagoras pointed to the door on the left. There were a bunch of plus and minus signs

painted on it, circling the words *Give and Take.*
"Step right in," he said.

"Will this take long?" I asked. "My mom's waiting in the car."

"Not long at all," he said. "Really, it will only take two minutes."

"Great." That was a relief, even though I wasn't sure how long two minutes was. I stepped inside the room with Benedict. It was smaller than my bedroom but a whole lot less messy. All I saw in it was a table with pads of paper and a bunch of pencils in a big cup. "So, we'll be right out?"

"Unless you fail the exit exam," Dr. Thagoras said. "Then it could take hours to get you out. Maybe even days."

CHAPTER
$1 \div 2 \times 10$

"**W**ait!" I screamed as the door swung shut. I couldn't figure out what time we'd get out if we were in the room for hours, but I knew my mom would come looking for us way before then. And that would not be good.

I heard a loud clank, like a big bolt had just slid into place. "Hey, wait. Don't lock us in!" I grabbed the door handle and yanked at it.

The door was locked. A hum came from the walls. I felt air rushing back into my head. Glowing bits of light swirled around me. Was that my math skills returning?

"Okay, 2 + 2 = 4," I whispered. Yeah, I could add.

There was a small screen in the center of the door, with a keypad below it. The screen flickered. Then a message appeared. A familiar voice read the message out loud. I wasn't happy when I realized that it sounded just like the robot.

"Add the numbers from 1 through 99. Enter the total. Hurry—you have two minutes." The word *hurry* flashed a bunch of times, and then the whole message vanished. A countdown clock replaced it. The display showed 1:59.

Benedict reached for the keypad.

"What are you doing?" I asked. There was no way he already had the answer. If he was a math genius, he'd kept that information a total secret from me his whole life.

"Using the calculator."

"That's not a calculator," I said.

"Sure it is. It has keys for the numbers."

"Yeah. And how are you going to add anything?"

"With . . ." Benedict didn't say another word. I guess he'd realized there was no plus sign or any other buttons for doing math. Beside the digits from 0 to 9, there was only one other key, with Enter on it.

The timer had counted down to 1:47. "Let's get to work," I said.

"How?"

I grabbed a couple of pencils from the table and two sheets of paper. I realized, outside of this room, I wouldn't have even been able to figure out how much paper to grab.

"Let's just do what it says and add the numbers." I started to write out the whole problem, "1 + 2 + 3 + 4 + 5," but I realized that would waste a lot of time. The display was now at 1:28.

"It's better to start with the higher numbers," Benedict said. "What's 99 + 98? Are you sure that's not a calculator? It would really help to have one."

I figured it would be easier to add the smaller numbers first. But either way, it still looked impossible to finish the problem before time ran out. The counter was down to 1:05. It didn't matter whether we added from 99 down to 1, or from 1 up to 99. There was no way I could do either of those things quickly enough to beat the timer.

"You start with 99. I'll start with 1," Benedict said. "We can each do half. Hey—that's actually a good idea."

"Wait!" As I thought about those two numbers—1 and 99—I felt a jolt shoot from my brain through my body. I wasn't used to having ideas hit me so hard. Especially not ideas as awesome as this one.

"What?" Benedict asked.

"Just a second. Let me think." *This might work.*

"We're never going to get out of here," Benedict said. He threw down his pencil. We're going to starve to death. And I don't see a bathroom. Do you see a bathroom? This room doesn't have a toilet!" He ran to the table, snatched up the pencil cup, and dumped out all the pencils. "Mine!"

I ignored him and wrote, "99, 98, 97, 96, 95" on the paper. Under that, I wrote, "1, 2, 3, 4, 5" so the large and small numbers lined up in pairs. I held the paper up for Benedict to see.

99	98	97	96	95
1	2	3	4	5

"Look." The pattern jumped right off the page. I felt a chill run through me as I realized my idea would really work.

"Look at what?"

"We can take pairs and add them. See, 99 + 1 = 100. So does 98 + 2. And 97 + 3. Get it? That makes it a lot easier. Every pair adds up to

100. Hundreds are easy to work with. How many pairs are there?"

"Why are you asking me?" Benedict said.

"Good point." I thought about it for a second, which was about all the time I could spare. The numbers from 1 through 49 matched up with the numbers from 99 down to 51. So there were 49 pairs. If the pairs added up to 100 each of those 49 times, that made a total of 4,900. I realized I also had to add in the 50, which didn't get paired.

As I rushed over to the keypad, I saw that the timer was down to 0:05. In five seconds, we'd be trapped.

"It's 4,950!" I shouted as I punched in the digits.

"You sure?" Benedict asked.

"No." I pressed Enter.

The lock clicked and whirled. The bolt slid free, and the knob turned.

"I changed my mind," I said as the door swung open. "I'm sure."

Dr. Thagoras was waiting for us on the other side. "Let's see, 9 + 3?" he asked.

"That's 12," I said.

"And 7 − 2?" he asked Benedict.

"It's 3," Benedict said.

"Whoa!" I shouted. "Did you say '3'?"

"Just kidding," Benedict said. "It's 5."

I looked at my watch. Altogether, we'd only been in the museum about ten minutes. It was nice to be able to add again. "We'd better get going." I didn't want to keep my mom waiting.

Benedict and I raced down the hallway.

Behind us, Dr. Thagoras called, "Wait a minute. I just realized something."

"I'm sure it's not important," I told Benedict as we headed up the stairs.

It's amazing how often I'm wrong.

CHAPTER
1 × 2 × 3

"Feeling better?" Mom asked when Benedict and I got back to the car.

"Absolutely," Benedict said.

I held my watch in front of Benedict's face. "Hey, if it takes fifteen minutes to reach your house, what time will we drop you off?"

He gave me the right answer and said, "I wonder how many telephone poles we'll pass on the way. Let's count them. One, two, three . . ."

I counted along. We got up to 92 when we reached his place. Before he stepped out of the car, he said, "If you bring 12 toy soldiers to school tomorrow, and I bring 15—"

"We'll have 27," I said.

Mom gave me a strange look. "You shouldn't bring toys to school."

"We're not. We're just practicing for our math test." Actually, I was enjoying the ability to do math. When we got home, I thought about studying for the test, but I figured the matheteria had pumped me so full of fresh math skills that I really didn't need to do any more studying. So I went over my social studies lesson instead since I sometimes have a hard time remembering all those facts and dates.

A while later, I heard Dad come home. Then Mom called me for dinner. My nose told me the good news even before I joined my parents and my little sister, Kaylee, at the table. It was takeout night. Dad had picked up chicken wings from Wingy Dingy. As it said on the side of the bucket, this was the *30-piece family pack!*

Dad took the tongs, grabbed a wing, and dropped it on his plate. Then he gave one wing to Mom.

That leaves 28, I thought. I was having fun doing math.

"Now we can divide the rest evenly." Dad handed me the tongs. "I heard you didn't keep your mother waiting at the mall. Good for you. You can take your share first, Logan."

I reached toward the wings. Then I froze.

"Go ahead, Logan," Mom said.

"Sure . . ." I stared at the bucket. There were 28 wings. I knew that. And there were 4 people at the table. But I had no idea what my share was. I could add and subtract without trouble. If I took a wing, there'd be 27 left in the bucket. If I took 5 wings, there'd be 23. If Mom put hers back with the 28, there'd be 29. But I didn't see how adding and subtracting could help me figure out my share.

"Is there a problem?" Mom asked.

As one part of my brain was telling me I should pretend there was an emergency and make a sudden dash to the bathroom, another part was actually thinking about math. I realized subtraction could actually help me, as long as I got everyone to play along. "We should take turns. That's fairer." I plucked one wing from the bucket and then passed the tongs to Kaylee.

"Yea!" Kaylee said as she grabbed a wing. "This will be fun."

We went around the table, taking one wing at a time, until they were all gone. I counted the wings on my plate. I had seven of them. So that was my fair share out of twenty-eight pieces. But I had no idea why. Even worse, I didn't know why I didn't know why, if that makes any sense.

I ate the wings, along with the green beans, mashed potatoes, and salad. Nothing tasted very good. All the food seemed to sit in my stomach like pieces of brick.

As soon as we finished dinner, I ran for the phone and called Benedict.

"We still have a problem," I said.

"I know. I was trying to study math so I won't wreck the ice cream party. All that multiplying and dividing stuff doesn't make any sense. I really don't understand how fractions work either."

"I'll bet we're still part numbed." I thought back to the matheteria. "There was a door on each side of the room. Remember? We went into the Give and Take Room. I guess it was just for addition and subtraction. The other room must be for multiplication and division."

"We have to go back," Benedict said.

"They're closed. We'll have to wait until tomorrow."

"School isn't going to be fun," he said.

"I have a terrible feeling you're right."

After I hung up the phone, I took out my math book to see for myself how bad it was.

Just like Benedict, all I knew how to do was add and subtract. If I had to take my share of anything tomorrow or figure out a fraction, I'd be in big trouble.

CHAPTER
(18 ÷ 3) + 1

The next morning, even before I reached the kitchen, I could tell by the clangs and clatters that Dad was whipping up a batch of pancakes. When I got there, he was beating some eggs in a metal bowl. "Hey, just in time to give me a hand." He nodded his head toward an empty measuring cup on the counter. "Pour 8 ounces of milk in there for me. Okay?"

"Sure." I felt a jolt of panic as I grabbed the milk from the fridge. But when I looked at the measuring cup, I realized I didn't need math for this. I just had to fill the cup up to the number 8. The cup could just as easily have been marked with letters of the alphabet or pictures of fruit.

"Great. Thanks," Dad said.

As I started to walk away, he added, "Now pour half of it into the mixing bowl."

Half? I came back and stared at the cup. *What's half of 8?* I had no idea. My only hope was to knock over the cup when I reached for it. That would make a mess, but it would also help keep my secret.

"Hurry up, I need 4 ounces," Dad said.

I felt the tension run out of my body like spilled milk. I knew 8 − 4 = 4. I'm sure Cypher would have something clever to say about the two fours. I didn't. I poured the milk and scurried upstairs. I figured I'd stay out of sight until it was time to eat. And then I'd keep my mouth stuffed as much as I could, so I wouldn't have to answer any questions.

"Is this enough?"

I turned and saw Kaylee holding out a handful of pennies and nickels. I didn't tense up at the question—I could count the coins. That was no problem now.

"Enough for what?" I asked.

"For six pencils at the school store," she said. "That's how many colors they have. Six. They cost 12 cents each."

Oh, no . . . The panic started to come back. I couldn't tell my little sister I didn't know the answer. *Think!* One pencil costs 12 cents. She wants six pencils.

"Do you really need more than one?" As I asked her that, I realized I didn't need to multiply. Just like I'd managed to divide the wings by subtracting over and over, I could add the cost of one pencil at a time, until I'd counted up the price of six of them.

"You can count to six, right?" I asked Kaylee.

"I can count to nine million zillion," she said.

"Great. I'll count the money for each pencil," I told her. "You count how many pencils."

That's how we figured it out. One pencil cost 12 cents. The second one added another 12 cents. That was 24. The third added 12, again, making 36.

"You need 72 cents," I told her. "And you have 85 cents. So do you have enough?" I knew the answer, but I thought it would be good for her to think about that part.

"Yeah! Thank you, Logan. You're so smart."

Wow—adding was like multiplying, except a whole lot slower. That was sort of like what Dr. Thagoras had told us—you could write any number just using slashes, or zeroes and ones, but it would be a lot longer.

I got through breakfast without any more math problems and then grabbed my backpack and headed for school. Benedict met up with me on the way.

"Last night was terrible," he said. "Who knew you needed so much math to play video games? Then I tried to play Scrabble with my dad. I was doing great until I played on a triple-word-score square."

"Class is going to be terrible if Ms. Fractalli wants us to work on multiplication," I said.

"We don't have math until the end of the day," Benedict said. "I've got it all figured out. You'll have to break your leg right before then. But at least you won't miss lunch. I'll help you to the nurse's office. And then we can go to the museum right after school."

"On my broken leg?" I asked. "Are you planning to carry me?"

"Good point," Benedict said. "Make it an arm."

"I'm not breaking an arm or a leg," I said.

"Finger?" he asked.

"No way."

"Fingernail?"

"No! Stop it. I'm not breaking anything. We'll get through this, somehow. It's not like you've never been in trouble. Come on, I want to get to class before Ms. Fractalli does."

I had a reason for that. When I reached my desk, I sat down and watched Ms. Fractalli come in. After she put her purse in the locker, she started to put her key on her desk, but then she went to the whiteboard and picked up a marker. She left the key on the tray. After she wrote a reminder about the test, she put the marker down right on top of the key. That was good. The more times I found her key for her, the better chance I had she'd take it easy on me if I ever got into big trouble.

Benedict was right that we didn't have our math lesson until the end of the day. But we were both wrong if we thought there'd be no math until then. I never realized how much math we did in school. Here are just some of the things we had to figure out *before* it was time for our actual math lesson:

In social studies, we had to figure out how many weeks Columbus's first voyage lasted. Luckily, I could do that.

For our science lesson, we watched a film about how they calculate the number of calories in different foods. It involved a lot of multiplying and dividing. Luckily, we didn't have to do the math ourselves.

We practiced the long jump in gym class. Each of us jumped three times. Our teacher, Mr. James, told us the average length of our jumps. Luckily, he did the math.

For lunch, they had tacos in the cafeteria. I wanted to buy three. Luckily, I'd already learned

I could add things instead of multiplying. Even more luckily, I didn't want twenty.

In art, we had to divide a circle into eight equal sections before we colored it. Luckily, I was able to watch the other kids at my table and do what they did, even though I didn't understand how I ended up with the right number of sections.

In music, we learned about 3/4 time. Luckily, Ms. Fourier likes to talk so much that she didn't have us do anything. Even so, my head was starting to hurt.

And then, unluckily, it was time for math. Ms. Fractalli grabbed a marker—but not the one that hid her key—and wrote a multiplication problem on the board: 127 × 12 = ?

"All right, class, who wants to solve the problem?"

Hands shot up around me so fast that I figured it had to be an easy problem. But all I could do was stare at the numbers. If I had to, I could add 127 to itself until I had 12 of them. But there's no way I could do that in front of the class. I looked around the room. Only two hands weren't up and waving—mine and Benedict's.

Maybe it was better to lose myself in a sea of raised hands than stand out as someone who didn't want to go to the board. I lifted my hand but made sure not to wave it around.

Ms. Fractalli looked at me. *Pick someone else,* I thought. *Please pick someone else.*

She looked past me. I relaxed. She spoke. "Benedict."

"Me?" he wailed from his seat two rows behind me.

"You." She held out the marker.

He shot me a terrified look as he walked up the aisle. It was bad enough he couldn't do the problem. It was terrible he'd fail in front of the whole class. He'd be reminded of it for the rest of the year.

Benedict was almost next to me now. He'd done something amazingly brave last year to save me from a dreadful punishment. It was my turn to save him. I could only think of one thing to do. It was risky, and it would definitely get me in trouble. But he was my best friend. There was no question in my mind. I'd do it.

I let out a loud yawn, stretched my shoulders back, and stuck my foot out as he went past.

CHAPTER
2 × 2 × 2

It worked. Benedict went sprawling.

"Hey!" he screamed when he got back to his feet. "You tripped me!"

"It was an accident." I shot to my feet. "I was stretching. You should look where you're going."

"You should keep your big feet under your desk."

"They're not as big as your head."

Benedict let out a roar and tackled me. We went rolling across the floor.

"Boys!" Ms. Fractalli shouted.

Benedict and I sprang apart.

"Go to the office. Both of you."

"That was fun," Benedict said when we got into the hall. "Did it look like I really tripped?"

"Totally."

"Good thing she doesn't know we play like that all the time."

"Yeah. I hope we didn't scare her too much." I knew Benedict wouldn't get hurt when I stuck my foot out. We play lots of games that involve pretend pushing, tripping, falling, and shoving. We just don't usually play them in the classroom. "Do you think we're in a lot of trouble?"

"No. We'll just get a lecture," he said.

He was right. I guess Principal Chumpski could tell that Benedict and I were friends and that the whole thing had been an accident followed by a misunderstanding.

We were warned and released.

We got back to the classroom just in time to miss the whole math lesson. Ms. Fractalli called us to her desk after the bell rang.

"I expected better behavior from you," she said.

"We're sorry," I said.

"Really sorry," Benedict said. "But we made up, and we learned a valuable lesson."

I kicked his foot to stop him from going too far. Ms. Fractalli seemed satisfied. She smiled, went to her cabinet, and reached into her pocket. The smile turned into a frown. "I seem to have misplaced my key," she said.

"I'll look." I hunted for a moment and then lifted the marker. "Found it!"

"Thank you, Logan," she said. "It's a good thing the principal didn't make you stay in his office. Well, I hope both of you are ready for the math test."

"We're totally ready. Math is all we've been thinking about," Benedict said.

Ms. Fractalli gave Benedict a funny look. I dragged him out of the room before he said too much.

After school, we took a bus right to the museum. Dr. Thagoras wasn't in his lab, but Cypher was. The robot rotated its head toward us.

"Uh-oh," Benedict said. "I don't want to get zapped again."

Neither did I. I didn't trust the robot. But I

knew what it was built to do. If I could keep it busy, it wouldn't hurt us. So I asked it a question. "Cypher, can you tell me about zero?" I remembered there was an exhibit upstairs about that.

That did the trick. Cypher started talking. About five minutes later, Dr. Thagoras walked in. "Ah, it's my two new math fans. You realize you ran out of here yesterday without all the skills you needed?"

"We sort of figured that out," I said.

"Can you fix us?" Benedict asked.

"I believe so," Dr. Thagoras said. "You'll have to go into the Repetition Room. It will restore your multiplication and division abilities."

He led us down the hall to the matheteria. When he opened the door to the Repetition Room, we saw a second door at the other end.

"This time, there are two rooms to go through," he said.

"Why?" Benedict asked.

"Numbers like patterns," Dr. Thagoras said. "So do mathematicians. In you go."

We walked through the first room into the second. "Good luck, boys," Dr. Thagoras said.

The door closed. Math flooded back into our heads in swirling numbers. I looked around. The far wall, opposite the door, and the walls on both sides were covered with multiplication problems. Tons of them.

"This can't be good," Benedict said.

CHAPTER
$9 \times 9 \times 9 \div (9 \times 9)$

Like before, there was a small screen in the door. This time, there was no keypad. But there was a message on the screen:

TOUCH THE ONE PROBLEM THAT HAS THE INCORRECT ANSWER. YOU HAVE FIVE MINUTES TO FIND IT.

A counter popped up under the message.

"You're kidding!" Benedict screamed. He

spun around, as if trying to find the best place to start or maybe to drill his way out of the room.

"Calm down. It won't give us a test we can't pass." I noticed there wasn't any pencil or paper. I was pretty sure I wouldn't be able to do most of the problems in my head. I walked to the back wall and looked at the problems in front of me. The first four were right at eye level:

$478 \times 18 = 8,604$

$27 \times 135 = 3,645$

$9 \times 18726 = 168,534$

$58 \times 72 = 4,176$

"Think," I said to Benedict. "There's no way we can check them all out by doing the math. Not in . . ." I glanced at the timer, "four minutes and forty seconds. So, how else can we check them?"

"I know I've said this before," Benedict said, "but WHY ARE YOU ASKING ME?"

I sighed and let my head slump forward. There were numbers on the floor. I saw a huge 9 by the door. Stretching out from that, crossing the floor, I saw:

18

27

36

45

54

It was multiples of nine. There was something familiar about that. I stepped back so I could see all of them. "Look," I said to Benedict, "do you see what's happening with the numbers?"

He moved next to me and looked down. "Why are you asking—wait! I see it. The numbers on the right go down one at a time."

"You got it." I could see it in my mind.

9

1**8**

2**7**

3**6**

4**5**

"And the other numbers—in the tens place—
go up by one." I could see that too.

9

18

27

36

45

"How does that help?" Benedict asked.

"I'm not sure. But it means there's a pattern."
I glanced at the timer. We'd used up a whole

minute. I thought about the pattern. And I realized why it seemed familiar. When we first met Cypher, he'd been ranting about numbers. One of the things he'd said was *9 × 8 is 72. Add the 7 to the 2, you get 9 again.* In each of the numbers on the floor, the digits added up to 9. I had a feeling that was true no matter how big the numbers got. If it went up on one side and down the same amount on the other, the total had to stay the same when you added the digits.

"That's it!" I scanned the walls so fast I got dizzy. "Look at the problems. In each one, there's a multiple of nine."

"Yeah, I see 18—that's 2 × 9. There's 27. That's 3 × 9. There's even 72." He moved like he was going to tap the wall by the 72, but I grabbed his wrist.

"Be careful. We're supposed to tap the problem with the wrong answer."

"Oops. That would be bad. Okay—so how does this help us?"

I pointed to the first problem: 478 × 18 = 8,604.

"Cypher was telling us about this. Look—if you add 8 + 6 + 0 + 4 in the answer, you get 18. Add the 1 and the 8 from 18 together, and you get 9. So that problem is correct. You start on the left wall. I'll start on the right one. Add up the digits in the answer. If you end up with more than one digit, add those digits too. You should always end up with 9, so if you don't, that's the one we have to tap."

We got to work. I was amazed at how every time I added the digits in the answer, it led me to 9. It might add up to 18 or 27 or a higher number, first, but those digits added up to 9. I realized I could even stop as soon as I knew I had a multiple of 9. After a minute, I discovered another shortcut. If I saw two digits that added to 9, I didn't even have to add them into the total. I could just cross them off in my mind.

I started to really zip through the problems. Like this one:

$434 \times 18 = 7,812$

I could see at a glance that I could toss out the 7 and the 2 on the outside, since they added to 9. The same with the 8 and the 1 in the middle. If I weren't in danger of being trapped, I would have really been enjoying this.

I realized a problem could still be wrong, even if the digits added to 9. They could scramble the digits in the answer. But that seemed like an unfair test. I just had to hope the test was fair. I finished the first wall. "How are you doing?" I asked Benedict.

"I'm about halfway done," he said.

"I'll do the back wall. Look for pairs you can toss out," I added.

If I could keep up my pace, we'd make it. But I was starting to get worried that I hadn't found the error yet. I hoped I hadn't missed it by mistake. There wasn't enough time to go back and double-check anything. I'd just reached the bottom of the back wall when Benedict said, "I got it!"

"Are you sure?"

"I think it's the one. Can you check it?"

"Yeah." As I was walking over, I saw that the

timer was almost down to zero. "Er—no! Go ahead. Do it. We only have three seconds."

Benedict tapped the wall. "I hope I didn't make a mistake."

I looked at the problem.

$72 \times 388 = 27{,}136$

There wasn't even time for me to add the numbers. But before the lock whirled open, I realized this was the problem we'd been looking for. The answer 27,136 was obviously wrong. The 7 and the 2 on one side added up to 9, and the 3 and the 6 on the other side also added up to 9. So the number in the middle, the 1, should have been a 9 or a 0.

"I hope the next room is easier," Benedict said as we walked through the door.

"Me too." There was a table in the middle,

like in the very first room. But when I saw the walls, which were covered with twice as many math problems as the room we were leaving, I had a feeling it wasn't going to be easier at all.

CHAPTER
4 × 25 ÷ (2 × 5)

While my eyes were glued to the problems on the walls, Benedict ran over to the table and shouted, "Look—there's a calculator."

"It can't be."

"Sure it can." He held it up. "This will be easy."

I saw that it had all the number keys and an Enter key, but no keys to add, subtract, or multiply. But it did have a Divide key. "That's no good. Division won't help us multiply."

I turned my attention to the problems on the walls. Each one had a screen and a keypad beneath it. The screens all showed 3:00. So we had to solve all the problems in three minutes. I looked at the ones to my left.

84 × 25 = ?

1,236 × 25 = ?

52 × 25 = ?

"They all use 25," I said. "There has to be something special about it."

"Wingy Dingy has twenty-five flavors of hot sauce," Benedict said. "And my Uncle Ralph just turned twenty-five. He had a big party at Wingy Dingy."

"I don't think that's going to help," I said. "What else?"

"I have no idea. We're going to be stuck here. I wish I'd brought a candy bar. Maybe I have some gum." Benedict shoved his hand in his pocket. Then his eyes got wide.

"What?"

"Quarters!" He pulled several coins from his pocket. "Numbers are one thing, but it's easy to think about money!"

"Right. A quarter is worth 25 pennies." My brain rushed ahead of my mouth as I tried to say what I was thinking. Quarters, pennies, and dollars swirled around in my mind.

It looked like Benedict was thinking the same thing. "There are four quarters in a dollar," he said. "And there are one hundred pennies in a dollar."

Benedict was right—money was easy to think about. I was so used to looking at four quarters and knowing they were worth a dollar. I needed to try to think about numbers the same way. "Since 4 × 25 is easy to figure out, we just have to see how many fours we have in each problem." I pointed at the calculator. "That's division! We can use this."

I looked at the first problem: 84 × 25. If I had 84 quarters, how many pennies would that be? I pointed to the calculator. "What's 84 ÷ 4?"

While Benedict was tapping the keys, I realized I could do that one in my head, one digit at a time. I started on the left, just as I would on paper: 8 ÷ 4 = 2. Then I moved to the right: 4 ÷ 4 = 1. So 84 divided by 4 was 21. That meant that 84 quarters was worth 21 dollars, which was 2,100 pennies.

I punched in the answer. The problem vanished from the wall, and the countdown timer on the screen was replaced by a check mark. One down, far too many to go.

We had 2:13 on the other timers. "We have to split up," I said. "That's our only chance. You use the calculator, and do all the ones with big numbers. I'll do the small ones." I figured I could do most of the problems in my head.

Benedict zipped around me, scooting from one problem to another, wiping out the longest ones. Each time, he punched in an answer, he shouted, "Score!"

I discovered another shortcut as I was speeding along. Instead of dividing the number by 4, I could divide it by 2 twice. It gave me the same answer, and for some of the problems, it was easier to do in my head. It's like, if you cut a pizza in half and then cut it in half again, you're really dividing it into four slices.

I had just finished the last of the easy problems when Benedict cried, "It's too long!"

I scanned the room and saw a sea of check marks. We'd answered almost every problem. Benedict was standing by the final one.

364,812,328,416 × 25 = ?

I looked at all those numbers. Then I looked at the timer. It was at 0:23. My stomach clenched like it had been divided by 4 a whole bunch of times, or divided by 2 a double whole bunch of times. There was no way I could solve that problem without a pencil and paper.

"We're doomed," Benedict said. "And this room doesn't have a bathroom either."

I thought about everything we'd been through so far. "It won't ask us to do things we can't do. I know it won't. It's all been fair. I just wish I had something to write with."

"You do," Benedict said, pointing to the keypad under the problem.

"But that's for the answer. No—you're right." I realized that the keypad wasn't just for entering the answer—it was also for writing down the answer, keeping track of each digit. I didn't need a pencil and paper. But I had to hurry. I only had seventeen seconds left.

"It's like when we do long division," I said. "I just have to start at the left and work my way across." I looked at the huge number again: 364,812,328,416. It was a lot longer than 84, but it worked the same way. All I had to do was break it up.

364,812,328,416

I started all the way to the left with 36. That

was easy enough: $36 \div 4 = 9$. I punched in the 9 and looked at the next digit.

36**4**,812,328,416

It was a 4. Piece of cake. I punched in a 1.

364,**8**12,328,416

Then I punched in a 2 for the 8.

364,8**12**,328,416

The next number was trickier: $12 \div 4 = 3$, but since I was skipping over the 1, I needed to put in a 0 before the 3. I punched in 03.

364,812,**32**8,416

The same for the next pair: $32 \div 4 = 8$. I punched in 08.

364,812,32**8**,416

364,812,328,**4**16

364,812,328,4**16**

I raced through the rest, typing 2,104.

I looked at my answer: 91,203,082,104. I'd solved the problem with six seconds left. I was about to hit Enter when Benedict grabbed my arm.

"Wait!" he shouted.

"Are you out of your mind?" I tried to yank my hand free.

"You forgot the two zeroes at the end. It's like 100 pennies. Remember?" He let go of my hand.

"Wow. You're right." I quickly tapped 0 twice, then hit Enter.

$364,812,328,416 \times 25 = 9,120,308,210,400$

The lock clicked open.

"Wow," I said again. "Good going. You saved us."

"Hey, when it comes to counting money, I don't make mistakes," he said. "Unless I'm numbed."

We staggered out. Dr. Thagoras was waiting for us. I wasn't happy to see that Cypher had joined him. I guess the new wheels allowed him to go where he wanted.

"Well done," Dr. Thagoras said. "I was confident you boys would succeed."

"I still know more than you do," Cypher said.

"Yeah, but you'll never be alive," Benedict said. "You'll never laugh at a joke. You'll never even feel anything. I feel all kinds of things. Watch this, you hunk of metal."

Benedict pinched the back of his own hand really hard. "Ouch! That was a mistake." He shook his hand and jammed it under his other arm.

I could swear I heard Cypher chuckle. But I didn't care. Getting multiplication and division skills crammed back into my head was exhausting. All I really wanted to do was go home and totally empty my mind for a while.

"You don't know everything," Cypher called after us as we headed out.

"Now, Cypher," Dr. Thagoras said, "nobody knows everything. Even you should know that."

"I know one thing," Benedict said. "We are totally acing that test tomorrow."

At that moment, I didn't see any way he could possibly be wrong.

CHAPTER
1 + 2 + 3 + 5

I felt great that evening. After dinner, I helped Kaylee with her math homework. It was cute watching her draw a circle around the bigger number in each pair. Her homework involved a lot more coloring than mine.

The next day, when it was time for math, Ms. Fractalli wrote 85 on the board. "This is the lowest average I will accept," she told us. "I'd be much happier if it comes out closer to this." She wrote 100. "But if the average score is at least 85, you will get ice cream sundaes."

I looked over my shoulder at Benedict, pointed at my chest, and mouthed the words *one hundred*.

Benedict tapped his chest and mouthed *110*.

I gave him a puzzled look. "Extra credit," he whispered.

I didn't know whether there'd be any extra credit problems, but I knew I was ready to blast through whatever our teacher threw at us. I was a flawless math machine, a fearsome number cruncher, and a tireless human calculator. Nothing could stand in my way.

I was so eager to start that I almost snatched the test right out of Ms. Fractalli's hand when she reached my desk. I already had my pencil clutched and ready.

Zip! I blew through the addition problems.

Zap! I knocked off all the subtraction.

Zim! I destroyed the multiplication.

Zoom! I shattered the division.

Huh? I stared at the next section.

After the regular arithmetic problems, I found myself facing this:

Tyler has seven pets. Some are chickens, and some are hamsters. If Tyler's pets have a total of eighteen legs, how many chickens does he have?

Uh . . . What . . . ?

I looked at the clock. My math skills and the shortcuts I'd figured out had let me knock off the first part of the test in record time, even after I'd double-checked each answer. But I had absolutely no idea how to solve this problem. I couldn't even start to think about it. I was pretty sure, before I'd been numbed, I would have been able to figure it out. But something was missing from my mind.

I read the next problem.

Maria has five shirts, two pairs of pants, and three pairs of shoes. How many possible outfits can she put together?

I let out a small moan. I should have been able to figure this out. But like with the first problem, I couldn't even think about any way to come up with a solution.

The next problem was no better:

Oliver has 50 feet of fence. He wants to make a rectangular garden. One side will be 12 feet long. How many square feet will the garden have?

It might as well have asked me to guess Oliver's middle name or his favorite kind of pie. I was totally clueless. I read the rest of the problems. I had no idea how to do any of them. I risked a glance back at Benedict. He was staring at his test like the paper had turned into a kidney.

The bell rang. We handed in our tests. "Did you get stuck?" I asked Benedict as we walked away from Ms. Fractalli's desk.

"It was way worse than being stuck. I was totally numbed."

What was going on? I glanced at the board, with the 85 on it. I tried to guess whether my total failure and Benedict's with the word problems would bring the class average below that number. It made me feel worse when I realized I didn't even know how to figure that out.

Ms. Fractalli was walking toward her locker. "If we ever needed to get on her good side, this is the time," I whispered to Benedict.

I waited until Ms. Fractalli realized she didn't have her key. Then I hunted around and found it where she'd left it, between two pages in the big dictionary.

"What's going on?" Benedict asked me as we left the school. "I thought we weren't numbed anymore."

"I don't know. But I hope Dr. Thagoras does. We'd better get to the museum right now."

CHAPTER
(2 × 3) + (3 × 2)

As soon as we reached his lab, I told Dr. Thagoras about the test.

"Oh, dear," he said. "I was afraid of that."

"Afraid of what?" I asked.

"There's a lot more to mathematics than just arithmetic," he said. "I was hoping you hadn't lost anything except your ability to perform basic calculations, but it appears you were very deeply and thoroughly numbed."

"I told you," Cypher said. "You don't know everything."

"Be nice," Dr. Thagoras warned the robot.

"What else is there?" Benedict asked.

"My word, that's an excellent question." Dr. Thagoras scrunched his forehead for a moment. His eyes darted back and forth as if he were watching a grandfather clock. Then he started listing things. "There are dozens of concepts and skills. Reasoning, estimation, rounding, exponents, logarithms, and lots more. Then there are the fields of math. Algebra, calculus, set theory, geometry, trigonometry, game theory, statistics, topology. It's almost endless." He chuckled and then added, "I was about to say it is infinite. But that is such a misused concept."

I stared at him for a moment before I spoke. "I'll never get all of that back, will I? Part of me will be numbed forever?"

"There might be one chance," Dr. Thagoras said. "You need to do something that allows you to grasp all of math, inside and out . . ."

"What are you talking about?" I asked.

He pointed to the wall behind him. "The ring on the outside was built before I started working here, so I don't know a whole lot about it. It's hollow. It was intended as an exhibit, but people found it far too confusing. I think you have to travel the Mobius loop, all the way around the inside of the ring." He got up from his stool and rushed down the hall. "This way."

We followed him back to the matheteria. He pointed at the far end, to the door marked

Maintenance.

"What's this about a loop?" Benedict asked.

"I assume you failed to watch the video in the lobby." Dr. Thagoras thumped the door. "As you may have noticed, the outer ring has a single twist in it. This makes it into a unique shape. If you put your hand on a wall and started walking, you'd have to go all the way around twice before you got back to where you started."

"I don't get it," Benedict said.

"Try it yourself with a strip of paper, sometime," Dr. Thagoras said. "Give one end a half twist. Then tape the ends together in a loop. That's called a Mobius strip."

Unlike Benedict, I had seen part of the video. But I still didn't see how a twisted strip of paper was going to help get us out of this mess.

Dr. Thagoras opened the door. Blue light spilled into the room.

"Wait." I looked over at the Give and Take and Repetition doors. When we'd gone into those rooms, we'd been in danger of getting trapped. Those had just been small rooms. This was a whole loop. "What's the risk this time?"

"I'm not sure," Dr. Thagoras said. "Nobody has ever done this."

"Trapped," Cypher said. "You'll be trapped forever." He laughed again.

"He's joking, right?" I asked.

"He's not programmed to joke," Dr. Thagoras said.

"Maybe we should just go home," Benedict said. "I mean, we can do arithmetic. That should be good enough."

"Remember when you thought we didn't need any math at all?" I said. "That didn't work out very well for us, did it?"

"I guess not," he said.

"Giving up now won't work either," I said. "We have to go."

"You're right," he said. "But why worry? There's nothing that can stump the two of us." He turned toward the open door and said, "Bring it on, Mobius. We're ready for you."

I started to go inside and then looked back. "Any idea how many problems there will be?"

"Well, you had one problem the first time and then two the next time," Dr. Thagoras said.

"What do you think comes next?"

"Three?" I guessed.

"Possibly. But I think four might be more probable," he said. "Remember, numbers like patterns. Starting with 1, you double it to get 2, and when you double 2, you get 4."

"It's a good thing this is the last time," I said. "I wouldn't want to go into a place with eight problems."

Benedict and I entered the loop. "I hope there aren't any more timers," he said.

Dr. Thagoras closed the door behind us. Numbers and symbols flooded back into my brain, along with other things I couldn't iden-tify. Some were just squiggles. Others looked like Greek letters. Suddenly, I knew how to solve those problems from the math test about pets, clothing, fences, and all of that stuff. Too bad I wouldn't get a second chance.

We were in a low, narrow corridor. It seemed pretty square—the floor was as wide as the walls were high. I guess we were inside the ring. There was a steel door blocking the path to the left, so we headed to the right. There was just enough light to see where we were going.

"Do you understand this twice-around thing he told us about?" Benedict asked.

I thought about the video, with the guy drawing a line on the side of the strip. It still didn't make much sense. "Not really. I hope it isn't on the test." I looked down as I walked. "Cool." My footsteps left green glowing marks on the floor, showing me where I'd been.

There was a slight tilt to the walls and the

floor. The farther we walked, the more we leaned sideways. After a while, everything tilted so much, the left wall became the floor and the ceiling became the left wall.

That's when we reached the first problem. There was a door ahead of us, with a keypad and a screen. Actually, there were two screens. One was lit. The other, above it, was upside down and dark. I read the question on the lit screen:

WHICH HAS MORE VOLUME,

A CUBE 50 INCHES TALL OR

A SPHERE 50 INCHES IN DIAMETER?

The keypad had two keys, labeled Cube and Sphere. We'd learned about area in math and had started to learn about volume. "Do you know how to figure out the volume of a sphere?" I asked Benedict.

"It's something with pi, right?" Benedict said.

"Yeah. But there has to be another way to figure this out." I pictured the cube. It didn't matter whether it was one inch or a million inches. I just had to picture a sphere the same size.

"Got it!" I said as the image in my mind gave me the answer.

"Me too," Benedict said.

I tapped Cube. The sphere would fit inside the cube, so it had to have less volume. I saw another way to think about it. If I started with a 50-inch-tall cube, I'd have to carve parts of it away to make a 50-inch-tall sphere.

"That was easy. We're one-fourth finished," Benedict said.

"Right. But if we miss any of the four, we're totally finished." I opened the door and kept walking. Once again, our right wall gradually became our floor. As soon as we got to the point where the floor felt level, we reached the next door.

And once again, there were two screens. I saw a problem on the lower screen and a keypad below it, with numbers, an Enter key, and a % key.

Benedict read the problem out loud:

A COIN WAS TOSSED 5,000 TIMES. IT LANDED WITH HEADS SHOWING 2,786 TIMES AND TAILS SHOWING 2,214 TIMES. ON THE NEXT TOSS, WHAT IS THE PROBABILITY OF HEADS?

"How are we supposed to figure that out?" I said.

Benedict pulled a coin from his pocket. "I'll start tossing. You keep track until we hit 5,000. It's a good thing there's no time limit."

"I don't think that's how we find a solution," I said.

Benedict flipped the coin and let it land in his open palm. "I guess you're right. Besides, it's not the same coin as in the problem."

"That's it!" I grabbed his wrist and pointed at the coin. "You're right—it *isn't* the same coin."

He stared at his palm. "It doesn't matter which coin we toss, does it?"

"It's a brand-new toss. That's the answer. It has nothing to do with what happened before. Five thousand tosses, five million, it's the same. All we need to know is the chance of heads on the next toss."

Benedict turned the coin over. "Two sides. Two ways it can land. So it's one out of two."

"Yeah, 50 percent. Go ahead. You do it."

Benedict put in the answer. "That's two," he said. "We're at 50 percent."

"Just like the coin." I opened the door and walked through.

"Wow," Benedict said. "Look at that." He pointed at the ceiling.

"Yeah, wow." I saw footprints up there, leading away. We'd started our loop on the other side of this door. Except the ceiling had become the floor as we moved through the twist. One more loop and we'd be back at this door for the final problem. I was beginning to understand what was so special about this Mobius loop.

Once again, we went halfway around before we came to the next door. Actually, I realized, it was the lower half of the first door we'd come to in the loop. The part that had been the ceiling then, halfway through our first time around, was now the floor, halfway through our second time around. Every time we went halfway around the loop, the walls and floor made a quarter turn.

The keypad under the lit screen had two buttons. One was marked with an A. The other had a B. I read the problem on the screen:

WHICH WOULD BE BETTER TO GET?

A. $1 A DAY FOR A WHOLE YEAR

B. 1 PENNY THE FIRST WEEK,

2 PENNIES THE SECOND WEEK,

4 PENNIES THE THIRD WEEK,

AND SO ON, DOUBLING THE AMOUNT

EACH WEEK FOR A YEAR

"That sounds like an easy choice," Benedict said. "I mean, one penny to start. How much could that end up being?"

"It could be a trick," I said.

"Or a double trick," Benedict said. "They make it sound wrong so you'll think it's right, but it's really wrong."

"It could be a triple trick," I said. "Or even a quadruple one."

"Oh, no, I hadn't thought of that." Benedict backed away from the door.

I didn't really think it could be a triple trick, but I couldn't resist seeing how Benedict would react. "Come on—let's stop guessing and figure it out."

I wondered how hard it would be to keep track of doubling the money and also adding in the total for each week. "I'll do the doubling, and you add it. Okay?"

"Go for it."

"Week one, 1 cent."

"One," Benedict said.

"Week two, add another 2 cents."

"And 1 + 2 = 3," Benedict said. "This is easy."

"Week three, add 4 cents."

"Then 3 + 4 = 7."

"Week four, add 8 cents."

"Then 7 + 8 = 15. It's almost a month, and it's nowhere near a dollar, yet," Benedict said. "And the other way, we'd get $365. That has to be the right answer."

"Hold on. I want to be sure. Where was I? Oh yeah. Week five, add 16 cents."

"That's . . . I lost track," Benedict said. "Let's start over."

"No. I don't think we have to. I guess 15 cents isn't very much, after four weeks. But it's still *fifteen times* more than we started with. I think the amount is going to grow so big that the answer will be obvious, even if we don't bother adding the totals. Let's start doubling, and see what we get."

I held up my fingers, one at a time, to help me keep track: "1, 2, 4, 8, 16, 32, 64, 128." I looked at my hands. We'd finally passed a dollar on the eighth week. I kept going.

"Then 256." I paused for a second, wondering whether I could do the next one in my head. But I saw that I could ignore the 6 at first and just double the 250. That was easy—250 doubled was 500. Double the 6 and add it back in, and the result was 512.

I kept going. "Next is 512." I had all ten fingers up now. I nodded at Benedict, who took over with his fingers as I counted. But I didn't think we'd need to go much further. We were already up to $5.12 on the tenth week.

"Then 1,024. That's $10.24. Then 2,048. That's $20.48."

"Wow, that's already way more than $7 a week, which you'd get if you took a dollar a day," Benedict said. "We're only at the twelfth week, and we're not even adding up the total from each week. You're right—it's going to get huge."

I could have stopped right there, but I was curious. Rounding the $20.48 to $20, just to make the math easier, the weekly payment would grow to $40, $80, $160, and so on. And that was just the fifteenth week. I had no idea how much it would be at the end of a year, but I had a feeling it would take a long time to even write the number.

"I guess it really was a double trick," I said.

"Yeah, the trick is to try to double your money as often as you can," Benedict said.

I pressed B on the keypad.

The door swung open.

"Last one's up ahead," I said.

"We're ready."

"I hope so." I was proud of how well we'd done, but I had a feeling the final problem might be four times harder than any of the others.

We walked along the second half of our second pass through the Mobius loop. We were now looking at the bottom half of the second door. We'd already done the problem on the top half during our first pass through the loop, when we'd been walking on the ceiling.

There was a screen. But there was no problem.

Instead of a keypad, there was a whole keyboard. I hadn't noticed that before, in the darkness.

"Welcome to infinity," a familiar voice said. "You have this much time to solve the problem."

Numbers started streaming across the screen, flowing faster and faster until they were a blur.

"I'm starting to not like this," Benedict said.

I didn't like it, either. I sort of knew what infinity was, but I didn't think I really understood it.

"You can solve the problem or remain in this infinite loop," the voice said.

"What's the problem?" I asked.

"A hotel has infinite rooms, each of which can hold only one guest. Every room is filled. So the hotel also has infinite guests. Do you understand, so far?"

"Yeah," I said. That didn't seem too hard to imagine, as long as I didn't think about it too closely. The rooms went on and on forever.

"I'm getting an infinite headache," Benedict said.

I shushed him and waited for the rest of the problem.

"Infinite more guests show up. How can you find rooms for all of them without asking any of the current guests to leave?"

"What?" I asked.

The voice repeated the question. Then it added, "Take your time. You are allowed to make infinite guesses."

Benedict stepped past me and typed: *Build more rooms.*

"Wrong," the voice said.

Benedict stepped away from the keyboard. "Well, that was the best I could do. Any ideas?"

"Not yet. But we've solved every problem. And we've done it using things we've known. We have to be able to do this one. What do we know about infinity?"

"It's big!" Benedict guessed.

"Yeah. But it's more than big. It's endless."

"Let's try that," Benedict said. He typed: *Put all the new people at the end, after the guests who are already there.*

"Wrong," the voice said. "There is no end to an infinite number of rooms already filled with an infinite number of guests. Nice try. Go on. You have infinite guesses remaining."

"Forget it!' Benedict said. "This is a trap. Dr. Thagoras and his robot want the two of us to stay here forever. I never did trust the two of them."

"Two . . ." I said. I thought about everything I'd learned or discovered about numbers and patterns and binary robots. "I have an idea." I wanted to think about it for a minute, because I wasn't sure how to write it out.

"Oh, man," Benedict said. "Having infinite time is worse than having a limit. The other way, it's over quickly. That's why they yank loose teeth. This way, you can suffer forever."

I went to the keyboard. Even though I was still sort of fuzzy about infinity, I felt I had a good idea of how to solve this problem. There was someone in every room. If we moved everyone up to the next room, putting the person in room #1 into room #2, putting the person in room #2 into room

#3, and so on, it would just empty the first room. That wouldn't give us infinite rooms. But if we moved everyone at once, that would do the trick.

I typed my answer: *Move each current guest into a room with twice as large a room number.*

"Huh?" Benedict said, looking over my shoulder.

"You put the person in room #1 into room #2, the person in room #2 goes into #4, the person in #3 goes into #6, and so on. You free up infinite rooms."

I could actually picture it. The infinite current guests would go into infinite even-numbered rooms. The infinite new guests would get the infinite odd-numbered rooms.

Guest in room: 1 2 3 4 5 . . .

Goes into room: 2 4 6 8 10 . . .

Freeing up room: 1 3 5 7 9 . . .

"That would never work," Benedict said.

Before I could argue my point, the voice said, "Correct."

The door swung open. We walked through and saw the very start of our footstep trail right in front of us. "We did it," I said to Benedict. "We finished the Mobius loop."

"Yeah, we did." Benedict looked like he couldn't believe it. "What are the odds of that?"

I shook my head. "I don't even want to think about it." I opened the outer door.

"Congratulations!" Dr. Thagoras said. "That should fix the problem for good, unless you find another way to get numbed."

"Thanks," I said. "I don't think you have to worry about that. We aren't planning to have any more conversations with robots."

Benedict walked over to Cypher. "Hold on. I have one more thing to say to you." He poked the robot in the chest. "Numbers are—"

"No!" I shouted.

"Awesome," Benedict said. "I love numbers." He leaned over and gave Cypher a hug.

Cypher said, "One plus one is two."

I dragged Benedict away from his new pal, and we headed out of the museum.

"Now, we just have to survive one more thing," he said.

"What's that?" I asked.

"Getting our math tests back tomorrow. That's not going to be fun."

"Not fun at all," I said. I could already imagine the look of disappointment in Ms. Fractalli's eyes.

CHAPTER
52 ÷ 4

"**Y**ou really better watch where she puts her key," Benedict said when we got to the classroom. "We're going to need every little bit of help we can get."

"For sure. And she's not the only one who isn't going to be happy." I looked around at a room full of classmates who were probably already trying to decide whether to go for hot fudge or butterscotch. "Everyone's going to be angry with us when they figure out who ruined the average."

My hopes drooped even lower when Ms. Fractalli walked into the classroom. She unlocked the cabinet, but then she took the old lock off and put another one in its place. The new one looked like some kind of combination lock with a row of buttons on the front.

"That's the end of that," I said to Benedict.

"All we can do is wait for our doom," he said.

We waited all morning, wondering when she'd tell everyone the bad news. But she didn't say a word.

Finally, when the class headed out to recess and lunch, Ms. Fractalli said, "Logan, Benedict, I need to speak with you."

Oh no. I looked over at Benedict, who was looking at me. I think we both gulped, trying to swallow. We walked up to Ms. Fractalli's desk.

"I don't understand your tests," she said. "You both did perfectly on the first part and terribly on the last. The word problems counted for half the grade. Your scores dragged the whole class down below 85 percent. Can you explain this?"

Again, I looked at Benedict and he looked at me. I waited. He was really good at coming up with excuses.

"No explanation?" she asked. "I'd love to give you another chance, but I can't without a good reason."

"My mind sort of went blank," I said. "I lost my math skills. But I think they came back."

"Mine too," Benedict said.

"I guess I'll have to wait until the next test to find out," Ms. Fractalli said.

She got up from her desk and went to the closet. I turned toward the door. "We're doomed," I said to Benedict.

"Everyone is going to be angry," he said. "We might have to move. I have an uncle in Argentina. I've heard they have good steaks down there. You can come. He has lots of room."

Behind me, I heard a rattling sound. I looked over my shoulder. Ms. Fractalli was yanking at her new lock.

"What's wrong?" I asked.

"I was afraid I'd lose the piece of paper with the instructions, the way I was always losing the key, so I put it in my purse," she said. "Then I locked my purse in the cabinet, as I always do."

"You didn't memorize the combination?" I asked.

She shrugged. "I didn't get a chance to memorize it or even look at it. I was up pretty late grading the tests."

"Let me see." I liked playing with locks.

"It's hopeless," she said. "There are too many combinations."

I lifted up the lock and looked at it. There were five buttons on front, labeled A, B, C, D, E. "How does it work?" I asked.

"I'm supposed to push some of them in," she said. "But I don't know which ones or how many."

"I can get a saw," Benedict said. "Yeah—a power saw. Or those giant pliers they use on cars. Wait! Better idea! We could go to the high school and get some hydrochloric acid from the chemistry lab. That will eat right through it."

He kept talking, but I stopped listening. The lock had all of my attention. I knew there were letters on it. But it reminded me of the kind of number problems we'd solved at the museum.

"It's binary!" I shouted as the answer hit me.

"Cool," Benedict said. He stopped talking and looked over my shoulder. "Yeah, you're right."

I turned toward Ms. Fractalli. "If there was just one button, you'd only have two choices. Right?" I pushed down the button with A on it and then popped it back up.

"And two buttons would only give you four choices," Benedict said.

"For sure," I said. It was definitely like the binary numbers we'd learned about. "And three buttons would be . . ."

"Eight!" Benedict said. "Like Dr. Thagoras's light switches."

I held up my right hand and stuck out one finger at a time, doubling the number with each new finger.

Pinkie.

"Two."

Ring finger.

"Four"

Middle finger.

"Eight."

Benedict and Ms. Fractalli joined in.

Index finger.

"Sixteen!"

Thumb—my whole hand was spread wide.

"Thirty-two!"

"That's not a lot at all," Ms. Fractalli said. "I

should have realized it right away."

"Sometimes, we all forget our math skills," I said. I thought about those pennies that doubled every week for a year. It's a good thing the lock didn't have fifty-two buttons. Or even ten.

I started pushing the five buttons, going through the thirty-two possible combinations:

up-up-up-up-up

up-up-up-up-down

up-up-up-down-up

up-up-up-down-down

up-up-down-up-up

up-up-down-up-down

up-up-down-down-up

up-up-down-down-down

I tugged on the lock after each combination. I hoped I wasn't missing something. It seemed too easy. But then, after more than twenty attempts, I tried

down-up-down-up-down.

The lock pulled open.

"I did it!" I shouted.

"Logan, that was wonderful," Ms. Fractalli said.

I noticed that the A, C, and E were pushed down. "Ace," I said. "I'll bet you'll never forget that combination."

"And I'll never forget how you two helped me," she said.

"That's the power of two," I said.

She looked at the clock. "How'd you boys like another chance at the last part of the test?"

If anyone had ever told me I'd be cheering at a chance to take a math test, I never would have believed it. But I was sure cheering then.

"Ready?" I asked Benedict as we walked back to our desks with new copies of the test.

"Let's ace this," he said.

"Shhh," I said. "That combination is a secret."

But when Ms. Fractalli graded our tests, that's exactly what we did. Benedict and I aced it, saving our grades and the ice cream party.

And wouldn't you know it, when the time came for the party, we both ended up getting brain freeze again. But at least, this time, we didn't get numbed.

David Lubar has written a fairly large, though finite, number of books, including *Punished!* and *Hidden Talents*. He's always enjoyed math, but he never dared write a book about it until now. The chance to send Logan and Benedict on another adventure was just too tempting for him to resist. He lives in Nazareth, Pennsylvania, with his wife and various felines.